Listening to the Mukies

and Their

Character Building Adventures

By
Robert Bohlken, Ph.D

Illustrated by
Michele Veasey

Snaptail Press
Division of Images Unlimited
Maryville, Missouri

All inquiries should be addressed to the publisher at:
Snaptail Press
Division of Images Unlimited Publishing
P.O. Box 305
Maryville, MO 64468
imagesun@asde.net   www.imagesunlimitedpub.com

Cover character illustrations: Michele Veasey
Cover design: Dunn+Associates
Interior illustrations: Michele Veasey
Book design: Lee Jackson

ISBN 0–930643–15–1
First Edition

Library of Congress Cataloging–in–Publication Data

Bohlken, Robert L.
    Listening to the Mukies and their character building adventures /
written by Robert Bohlken; illustrated by Michele Veasey.– – 1st ed.
        p. cm.
Summary: Presents eight stories set in a primitive society in which the usually optimistic and happy Mukies work together to solve problems. Includes questions designed to improve listening skills and teach such values as cooperation, understanding, and respect.
    ISBN 0–930643–17–8 (hardcover) – – ISBN 0–930643–15–1 (softcover)
  [1. Conduct of life– –Fiction. 2. Values– –Fiction.] I. Veasey, Michele, ill. II. Title.
PZ7.B635825 Li 2003
[Fic]– –dc21

                              2002013868

10 9 8 7 6 5 4 3 2 1

Printed in the United States of America

Contents

Foreword

These noble and strong yet humble and compassionate characters have the ability to teach all of us lessons about relationships. The gregarious yet warm Mukies' ability to listen enables them to solve problems demonstrating the value listening has in our everyday lives. These stories should empower children to use their ears and their hearts to become responsible citizens within their communities.

Dr. Bohlken has developed clever characters sure to warm the hearts of children as they learn why listening to others is highly valuable. These stories and lessons should prove highly valuable to anyone dealing with young children. This book has the potential to make a real difference in children's lives. Forget sports figures, Mukies are the real heroes! Too bad all children don't have Michael or Millie Mukie influencing their lives. These clever creatures certainly show that through being open-minded and truly listening to one another we can cope with current issues such as racism, violence, and aggression.

The Mukies demonstrate the value of cooperation, but above all, whether listening to ourselves or to friends and family, the Mukies continually reveal the value of effective listening. Despite our inevitable mistakes, listening is the key to our success.

> Kimberly Batty-Herbert, M.A.
> President, International Listening Association
> Professor, Clovis Community College, Clovis, New Mexico

Introduction

This series of eight short stories is intended to develop an insight into character building and enhance reading and listening skills. The stories demonstrate problem-solving techniques and create an opportunity to share attitudes, ideas, and feelings between adult and youthful participants. They address topics of self-esteem, prejudice, mutual understanding and respect, rights and responsibilities in a society, and peaceful co-existence. Each chapter focuses on a different theme.

The stories are intended to be read aloud, with an exchange of the reading role between adult and child. The reader should interrupt reading by asking the italicized questions and discussion of the answer should follow. The reading aloud of the stories and the interaction of reader and listener are as important as the messages presented.

Research indicates that only sixty percent of middle school students engage in conversations of fifteen minutes or more duration with their parents on a daily basis. Twelve to twenty minutes appears to be the optimum time for an in-depth conversation involving attending, listening, and responding in an exchange of ideas and feelings. It takes this amount of time to develop topics that require thinking beyond the practical verbal exchanges at home about wearing apparel, food, and future plans; and at school, the topics of assignments, co-curricular activities, and providing information about a subject.

The students report that a major problem with extensive communication with parents is the lack of common topics and interests. Some common student statements are "We have a generation gap." "We have little common interests." "We have very little to discuss."

This book is an attempt to encourage adults and children to share thoughts, ideas, and feelings. The stories, set in a primitive society, are intended to serve as a basis for discussion. Simple parables are found throughout the stories that provide opportunities for youth and adults to exchange ideas and discuss common interest material. The review and activities at the end of each story help enhance the conversation and create mutual understanding.

The preferable communication situation for sharing these stories is at a table with reader and listener comfortably seated about two feet apart on the same chair level and slightly facing each other. It is important that both participants have at least fifteen minutes of uninterrupted time to devote to the situation and nothing urgent scheduled immediately after the session causing participants to be mentally preoccupied. Needless to say, the communication should take place in a quiet environment without noise distraction of others or media such as recorded music, radio, or television.

As with any communication situation, a purpose for the communication needs to be established by both communicators. The main purpose for this communication exchange is to establish a relationship through gaining an understanding of each other's thoughts and attitudes toward philosophical questions.

The messages presented in these stories are very much influenced by the creed and principles of the Optimist International Organization. The author is a life member of this organization and is actively involved in youth activities sponsored by the organization. These activities provide insight into the thinking and behavior of youth at the age for which these stories are intended.

The techniques and procedures for reciprocal listening and problem-solving dialogue have been influenced by the author's professional communication training and his association with communication associations, especially the International Listening Association. Listening, the most important skill in establishing interpersonal relationships, is the least taught of the language skills.

The introductory section, "Meet the Mukies," sets the stage for understanding the way the members of this society looked, acted, thought, and behaved. It describes their physical characteristics, optimistic attitudes, simple life, and primitive society. (The word "Mukies" is pronounced with a long u). Although they are different from us in appearance and outlook, they experience many of the same problems and have the same concerns we have in our society.

To my family and friends
for their encouragement

Meet the Mukies

In the land of "oohs" and "ahhs" there once lived a community of Mukies. Now, Mukies were strange looking creatures, with short, large immobile arms that ended in stubby hands and fingers. Their short stout legs were knee-less and their broad feet had tapered toes pointed outward from the body. They had stocky bodies, which were connected to their head without much of a neck at all. Their body hair was brown in color with black tips and was coarse and spiky in nature.

They had round heads, big protruding saucer eyes, bow shaped lips and mouth, and a button nose. Their pointed ears looked like milkweed pods.

The Mukies physical features and build made them slow and deliberate in their movements. They were very awkward and clumsy, but they were a bright and happy group.

What the Mukies lacked in physical dexterity, they had two-fold in heart and spirit. They were too loyal for anger, too happy for worry, and too confident for fear, at least most of the time.

They were an optimistic group of quick witted, predictable, and caring individuals. They worked and played hard together as a community seeking the best for all.

The Mukies were non-carnivorous, that is, they didn't eat meat. Their vegetarian diet consisted of berries, parsnips, and grains, with melilot their favorite. They also really, really liked bee honey.

Each community was governed by the elders of that community. They had no national or state governments. The best was expected of each Mukie and they accepted only the best from each in the community.

Their society was much more primitive than ours but they had many of the problems we have today. The stories that follow present some of these problems and give us an opportunity to better understand ourselves through the Mukies' experiences and adventures.

Theme: "An Ounce of Prevention" demonstrates the problem-solving process and some of its influences. It also indicates that the prevention of problems is better than dealing with them after they occur. Throughout this series you will be involved in problem solving and hopefully you will use the process outlined below in helping you solve your own problems.

In families and communities, effective solutions to common problems evolve through the problem-solving process. This procedure consists of determining (1) the nature of the problem, (2) the causes of the problem, (3) the possible solutions, (4) the best solution, and (5) how to put the solution into effect. But, often times a step in the process is overlooked or more likely, personal characteristics influence the decision-making process. Such personal characteristics as perceived power, prestige, intelligence, gender, and physical appearance influence the process.

Chapter 1

An Ounce of Prevention

One particular community of Mukies was called Mukieville. These Mukies lived in a community on a high bank above a stream of water. From this stream they got their necessary water for drinking and cleaning.

They had carved into the bank a curving path upon which to carry their water from the stream to the village. You see, the Mukies stayed away from the water as much as possible. Because of their physical structure, they were very, very poor swimmers.

How do physical characteristics influence society and personalities?

The Mukies favorite food was melilot. In the summer, they would go to the melilot field at least once a day. They even dried and stored melilot for their winter use. Melilot was their very, very favorite food.

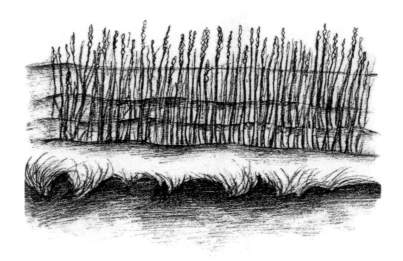

Fortunately, a big field of melilot was nearby. But, unfortunately the melilot field was on the other side of the deep stream, the opposite bank from the village.

The Mukies built a bridge to the melilot field by putting a narrow log reaching from their bank to the bank across the stream. However, at times, especially on windy days, crossing the narrow log bridge was dangerous. This is where they encountered their problem.

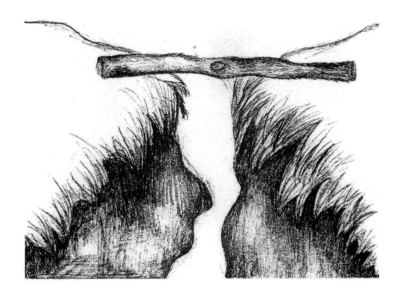

You see, the awkward Mukies were apt to fall into the water stream, be carried away by the current and drowned while others stood by helplessly. Now the Mukies realized they had a problem, but how was it to be solved?

They really couldn't move their village, but melilot was their favorite food and it was on the other side of the river. They couldn't tell when one of them would lose their balance or when a strong wind would blow one of them off the log into the stream. Remember, Mukies were too happy for worry, but they were also awkward.

What do you think they should do?

After the second Mukie in three weeks fell from the bridge into the stream, the Mukies held a village meeting. Marvin Mukie stood up at the meeting and in his confident voice said, "We have to find ways to rescue our fallen brothers and sisters from the stream!"

The other Mukies quickly agreed "rescue" was the answer. "We will need to invent rescue equipment!" said Mylon. "Yea," said Marlyn, "we will have to save them quickly, but I know we can do it."

Millie Mukie had an idea although she didn't say anything. But, as an optimistic Mukie, Millie didn't criticize Marvin's solution to this problem.

Should Millie have spoken out and expressed her idea?

The Mukies devised all types of rescue equipment. They made a net of vines and stretched it across the stream to prevent the fallen Mukies from floating away. They made a hollow vine circle on a rope that would float and could be thrown to the drowning Mukie.

19

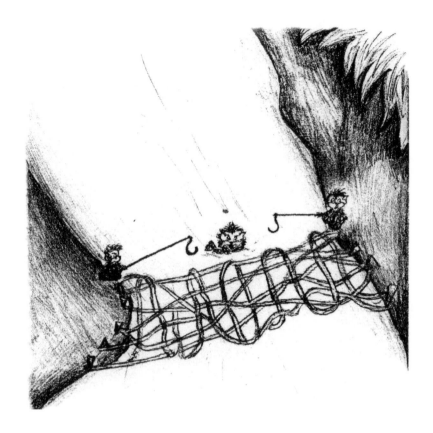

They devised long poles with hooks on them, so they could hook the drowning Mukie. They even established a rescue team which stayed by the stream waiting for a Mukie to fall from the narrow log bridge.

The elaborate attempts to rescue fallen Mukies failed! Myron Mukie fell from the narrow bridge. The alarm was sounded; the rescue team sprang into action.

"I'll hook him," shouted Mello Mukie. "Here Myron," yelled Mildred Mukie as she threw the circle of vine at Myron. "Secure the net," hollered Mervin, "he's coming down."

The rescue squad acted promptly with their hooks and nets, but Myron was so badly hurt by the devices used to save him, he died at the scene. It was a very sad situation for the Mukies.

What should the Mukies do now?

The village elders decided to call another meeting. At this meeting Millie Mukie stood up and said, "Let's forget our mistakes of the past. We need to prevent these accidents from happening rather than rescue our brothers and sisters after the accidents happen."

Mello Mukie stood up and said, "Good idea, Millie! Let's see how we can prevent these accidents."

Millie continued, "One of our forefathers once said, 'An ounce of prevention is worth a pound of cure.' We know what the problem is, but we need to understand what the causes are so we can prevent this from happening again."

The other Mukies all cheered in approval of Millie's comments.

Mello said, "The major cause is the wind. When it blows hard it knocks us off the bridge."

Marlin said, "I believe the bridge is too narrow!"

Murphy added, "We have nothing to hold onto so we can keep our balance when the wind is blowing ."

Mario suggested that the Mukies lacked training in balancing themselves on a narrow log.

Millie interrupted the conversation that evolved from Mario's suggestion by saying, "We now have the causes of the problem; we need to have some possible solutions."

Mario stated, "We need to train ourselves to improve our balance."

Myron said, "We need to prevent Mukies from crossing the bridge when the wind is blowing."

Millie stated, " I think we need to widen the bridge with another log."

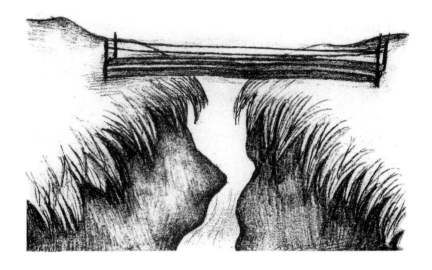

Marvin suggested using ropes as handrails.

What do you think they should do to prevent more accidents?

After some discussion about the advantages of each possible solution, Millie suggested, "Let's widen the log bridge to three logs and put on rope handrails."

The Mukies all agreed with Millie that this was the best solution. They then went about finding the extra logs and rope.

After widening the bridge and adding the handrails, no more Mukies fell from the bridge. The rescue team no longer sat around waiting for an accident to happen. Their problem was solved and they were again living their lives optimistically, and with positive and happy attitudes.

To Review:

1. What steps do you remember of the decision-making discussion?

2. Why is it important to explore many different ways to solve a problem?

3. What are the differences between a conversation and a discussion?

4. What kind of training do you think the Mukies would have needed to improve their balance?

5. Is group leadership via discussion always the best way to solve a problem?

6. Why do some people speak out in a group while others remain silent?

Activities:

1. In small groups, decide on a problem and go through the decision-making process. The problem might be:

> How can a family have at least one meal together on a daily basis?

> How can I find time to watch television and get my report finished?

> My former best friend won't talk to me. What should I do?

> I need $30.00 to buy... but I don't have the money.

Consider what caused the problem or why it is important to you. Ask questions and consider consequences of various responses. Think of possible solutions, choose one, try it out, and evaluate the results. Was this a good decision?

2. Survey your family or friends to determine who listens most effectively to whom, where they listen most effectively, when they listen most effectively, and what influences them most when listening effectively. Consider the speaker, the topic, the listener him/herself, distractions such as television, noise, etc.

3. Role play Millie and Marvin in a situation in which each is attempting to get the community to listen to them.

4. Brainstorm to determine the most urgent problems within your family or school.

Theme: "The Happy but Unhappy Mukie" provides the opportunity to explore the concepts of self-esteem, contentment, and happiness. It points out ways we let others influence us, such as mass media, the internet, and those with whom we associate.

It looks at empty promises made by naïve sources with misunderstood motives. It illustrates how discontentment can be created and spread, especially among those we love. It points out how temptations and promises of a better life are seldom reality.

This story helps us understand that self-esteem, the basis for happiness, must come from within each of us, and we must be self-directed. One needs to listen to others, but it is most important to listen to oneself.

Chapter 2

The Happy but Unhappy Mukie

A long time ago in the land of Mukies there lived a Mukie farmer named Marvin. Now Marvin owned and farmed enough land to support his wife and three children comfortably. He and Millie, his wife, worked hard. They found satisfaction in their tasks, especially when it came time to harvesting melilot, the Mukies' favorite food.

Marvin and Millie took pride in their farm and their family. Oh yes, sometimes there were rough times when the melilot didn't grow as well as it should. Sometimes there were even disagreements among the family members. Or sometimes the little Mukies misbehaved; like one day Michelle Mukie, the youngest Mukie, ran off and got lost. But all in all, the Marvin Mukie family was content.

What do you think contentment is?

In those days, there were wandering Mukies who moved from place to place staying in one area for only a short time. These wandering Mukies, few in number and traveling alone, were viewed by the Mukies, especially the rural or farmer Mukies, as wise.

They were wise in the minds of farmers because the wandering Mukies had been places and had seen lands far and wide that the farmer could only dream about. The farmers would invite the wanderers for a meal and to spend the night just to hear them tell about their adventures of all the foreign places they had traveled.

How was the wanderer like our television, internet, and radio?

One night an old, weary traveler appeared at Marvin Mukie's door. Marvin invited him in by saying, "Come, share a meal and spend the night."

The old wandering Mukie replied, "I would be delighted."

After dinner the entire family sat around on the floor of their hut listening to the old Mukie telling about the wonderful sights and sounds of far away lands. The "Old One" told of beautiful lands where the sun shone warm all the time and gentle rains helped melilot grow dark green and very tasty.

After hours of storytelling, the children and Millie went to bed, but Marvin insisted the old Mukie continue. The Old One now was telling about far away places he had not been, but he had heard about from very "reliable" and "good" sources.

The Old One said, "I've heard of a place that lay between a gentle stream and rolling hills where one could find 'true' contentment and happiness. This place is paradise where everyone is truly happy all of the time. This place is free from cares and responsibilities."

Marvin asked, "How do they know they are happy?" The Old One replied, "You'll know you are happy when you find this place."

Do you think a place can provide happiness? Can happiness be found in a drug?

Marvin Mukie went to bed that night no longer a contented person. He now viewed himself a poor, unfortunate person who had missed his opportunity for "true" happiness.

Marvin slept very little that night as he thought of ways he might rid himself of his cares and responsibilities. He wanted to seek true joy and contentment and happiness beyond the small world that had been his life and love for many years.

Once a contented person, Marvin now became disheartened and disappointed. He sought things beyond what he was and what was his. He gave in to empty promises based on his faith in the Old One's imagination.

Do you trust all the people you listen to?

Before the morning's dawn had broken, Marvin awakened Millie to repeat the story of the old wanderer. Millie listened in silence. She did not share Marvin's excitement. She waited for Marvin to finish. When he had finished the story he said he, too, would go in search of real happiness, and when he found it he would come back for Millie and the kids.

Millie softly smiled as tears slowly slid down her cheeks. She said, "Marvin, you are our happiness, and hopefully we are yours. Please don't leave us in search for that which is beyond all expectation. Happiness is in people not a place."

Do you agree or disagree? Where do you find happiness?

Marvin did not argue; he turned and walked away. Now, Millie also was sad and discontented, for, you see, she now felt she had failed Marvin's expectations. Unhappiness, like happiness, is catching or contagious. Millie did not know what to do. Marvin's contentment had to come from within, and only he could recognize it.

Who do you think Marvin should listen to?

Discontented and frustrated, Marvin walked down to a small stream of water to think about what he should do. He looked down at a small pool of water that had collected in the stream. Marvin saw his image as if the pool were a mirror or looking glass. Then a leaf from a nearby tree fluttered down and fell on the surface of the pool. The falling leaf caused ripples on the surface of the pool and distorted the reflected image of Marvin.

Have you seen your reflection in the water? Are you pleased with what you see?

As the ripples and distortions of his face began to clear, Marvin thought to himself, "I am the one I need to listen to." Speaking his mind, Marvin said:

When life's choices come your way
Listen to what others have to say
But when all is said and done
Look into a mirror and listen to the reflected one.

When temptations are laid at your door
And promises are yours to take
Discuss the consequences and more
But listen finally to one in the mirror for your sake.

You may fool the world throughout the years
Others may admire you as you pass
But you'll suffer heartache and tears
If you don't listen to the one in the glass.

It is you alone who makes your choices
No matter what others may say or do
You may listen to other voices
But the voice of the reflected one
is most important to you.

Adapted from "The Man in the Mirror"
Anonymous

As Marvin continued to look at his reflected image, he thought, "If the old traveler had any idea where total happiness could be found, why is he telling me about it? Why doesn't he seek it for himself?"

Marvin then realized that happiness was working at what you like to do, having optimism and a faith in the future. It is sharing with others, and most of all, being loved and loving others.

With that, a happy thought came over him as he recognized he had all this right here at home among the rolling hills and a small stream of water. He didn't need to seek a place elsewhere. At last he understood that happiness came from within caring people.

What makes you happy?

Marvin smiled as he looked at his reflected image in the pool because Millie and the Mukie kids had joined him at the streamside. There reflected, the four of them were the images of happiness.

To Review:

1. Discuss what "happiness" and "contentment" mean to each participant.

2. Discuss the saying: "Grass always appears greener on the other side of the fence."

3. Discuss several reasons why Marvin should be content with his life and family.

4. Discuss why Marvin would believe the old wanderer and even think of leaving.

5. Discuss ways you are influenced in your life. What makes the greatest difference? Is it family? Friends? Television? Internet? Magazines and newspapers? The shopping mall?

6. Why is it most important to listen to yourself?

Activities:

1. List the sources of information that are available today. Which ones are most believable for world news? for moral and value issues? for character models?

2. Role play the old wanderer and Marvin if the promised land contained diamonds or material wealth.

3. Role play the conversation Millie and Marvin may have had if the situation had developed in your home.

4. Discuss the rights and responsibilities of family members in making a happy home.

5. Role play family members when they learn that one of the family has sought escape throught the use of alcohol or drugs.

6. Role play family members when they learn that the mother or father no longer want to be a part of the family.

Theme: The Mukies, like humans, in attempting to establish relationships with others, go through a process of weighing the advantages and the disadvantages of the relationship. Some take a pessimistic perspective and avoid the risk involved. Others try to gain friendship and fellowship through indirect action.

As a society, the Mukies depended on trust of one another for the benefit of all. In this story, distrust of the other's motives could prevent a new relationship from developing and cause unhappiness. Cooperation vs. selfish aggressiveness and challenge create an interesting situation.

Chapter 3

Crossing the Line

Micheal Mukie was small for his age, but his size did not call attention to itself. He was a very optimistic and happy Mukie. Micheal truly enjoyed the companionship of others his own age, and he was just as enthusiastic about the success of others as he was about his own. In fact, Micheal was so optimistic, happy, and complimentary of others that some envied him to the degree of aggression.

Do you know someone who is envied for his or her optimism and apparent happiness?

Micheal and his parents had just moved to a new neighborhood into a hut that had belonged to his Grandparents. Soon after they moved in, Micheal went outside on the path in front of his parents' hut. He saw a large, stout, and tall (relatively speaking) Mukie coming out of his family's hut down the path. He appeared to be about the same age as Micheal. Mandred was his name, and he was not a happy or contented Mukie.

Mandred was a pessimist who believed others would take advantage of him if he wasn't defensive and aggressive. He asserted himself with his physical appearance and strength. As the Mukies used to say, "He likes to throw his weight around."

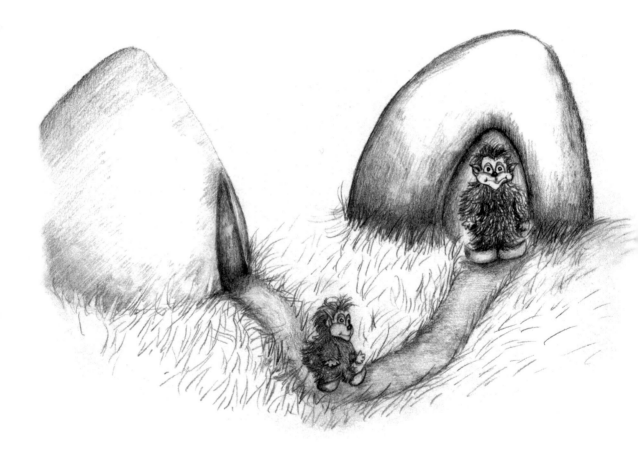

Micheal went to meet Mandred on the dirt path that ran in front of both their huts. He approached Mandred with a smile and said, "Hi! I'm Micheal. We now live in this neighborhood and I would like to become your friend."

Mandred scowled and questioned Micheal, "Why would I want to be friends with you? What good would it do me to be friends with a puny guy like you? I could beat you up in nothing flat if I had a mind to do so."

Looking down and away as he was crestfallen by Mandred's remark, Micheal replied, "I don't want to fight you or be your enemy! I just want a friend to share stuff, to hang-out with, and do things together...."

Mandred interrupted, "Do things with you? We have nothing in common. There is a big difference between you and me. There is a big line that separates us. You have nothing on your side of the line for me. What's in it for me?"

"Nothing," Micheal replied, "But I would care about you and I hope you would care about me. We could solve problems together and I could help you with your work."

Mandred caustically yelled, "What could you do to help me? You little punk!"

Micheal automatically retaliated, "You are a big bully!"

Does name calling ever help in a conflict?

Mandred yelled, "Oh yeah! What are you going to do about it, Punk Kid?"

Micheal looked Mandred in the eyes, turned away and went over to pick up a stick that had fallen on the path from a tree. He took the stick over near where Mandred was standing and in the dust of the path, he drew a line between them. Micheal stepped back on his side of the line, looked Mandred in the eyes and said, "Step over the line."

What does this gesture mean to you?

Mandred stared at Micheal and quickly jumped over the line and stood within three inches of Micheal. He looked down at Micheal and said, "I've stepped over the line. Now what are you going to do about it?"

Micheal looked away, turned, and moved away saying, "Now that you have crossed over, there is no line separating us, we have no differences and we can be friends."

Then Mandred began to laugh.

Do you think they will become friends?

To Review:

1. What qualities do you like in a friend? Can a parent or teacher be a child's best friend?

2. Why do friendships sometimes end? Can you ever outgrow certain friendships?

3. Why are friendships sometimes formed with others who have qualities you lack?

4. Does name-calling hurt? Is this a true statement: "Sticks and stones can hurt my bones but names can never hurt me?" Give examples of words that "hurt."

5. Who do you think will be more successful in life, Micheal or Mandred? Why or why not?

Activities:

1.Role play a possible conversation that occurred after Michael drew the line and said, "Now that you have crossed over the line, there is nothing separating us ... we can be friends."

2. Give examples of trust in the society. For example, many people trust their neighbor or banker or babysitter. Is this always good? Why or why not?

3. Give examples of times when trusting others was a poor decision. Give examples when trusting others was a good decision.

4. Create character highlights for story characters. After reading or telling a story, write the main character's name on the board or on paper. Describe the character's personality and actions. What are the traits you admire? Which ones do you dislike? What character would you want to be like?

5. Make up a poem about you and a good friend.

6. Write a positive comment about each of your friends and share it with them.

Theme: What do you think of when you hear the word "handicap"? The main theme of this story is: love and caring is more important than the negative meaning of "handicap", which exists only in the mind of the beholder. A handicap may be a blessing in disguise and be more beneficial than one's common capabilities.

This story provides insight into prestige, shame, and love within a family and a community. It illustrates that often what appears to be negative is actually positive if there is love and caring. Mutual respect is developed when nurtured.

Chapter 4

What Handicap?

The other Mukies of the community admired Midas and Minerva Mukie because they both were healthy, normal, and attractive. They both came from families who had lived in the community for a long time. In fact, both of them had ancestors associated with the founding of the community. In other words, whenever Midas and/or Minerva walked down the street, the other Mukies noticed them and they appeared to be "pace setters, fashion models, and social leaders."

Now, don't get me wrong, Midas and Minerva were not pretentious. It was just that they recognized their "station" or "status" in the community and wanted to fulfill their responsibility as role-models. They spoke to everyone and gave everyone a smile as if to say, "Everything is great for us and we hope the same is true for you."

Do you know people like this?

When Minerva became pregnant, the whole community was overjoyed with the thought of a "perfect" addition to the community. The community became "family" in anticipation of the birth of the "hero" to be. The blessed event of the birth occurred and news spread quickly.

Midas and Minerva became the parents of a tiny male Mukie named Mercury. The community was excited and it was said by the few who saw the baby's face that he had his parents' features.

The community hummed with gossip-filled excitement and anticipation of the "public" viewing. This child, Mercury, in the minds of the community was destined to be the leader of the community or perhaps the Mukies' Nation.

Is gossip always bad? Does one have to care about others to talk about them?

However, Midas, Minerva, and the midwife who assisted in the birthing soon realized that Mercury's feet were not large! Nor did they point outward like "normal" Mukies' feet; Mercury's small feet pointed straight ahead abnormally. Their "bud," Mercury, was different; he was "handicapped." He was healthy except for his feet, but his feet's shape and axis with his body were definitely different from "normal" Mukies' feet. They definitely called attention to themselves even while he was lying on his back.

What should be done about these abnormal feet?

Now, remember, there were no doctors or surgeons in the ancient Mukies' society. Midas and Minerva talked and listened to each other about the options in adjusting to Mercury's "handicap." They prayed and even sought the advice of the old traveling Wise One. The old Wise One admitted he had never before witnessed such a Mukie "handicap." He suggested that Mercury's feet and legs be wrapped and splinted to force the feet to a normal outward position. This splinting would be painful and could take years to correct if it ever did correct; no doubt, he would always be a "cripple."

Minerva was concerned about the reaction of the community to this poor mutinied "bud." The family, as well as their child, would lose their prestige and respect. She thought the Mukies may associate Mercury's affliction with a sign of past family sins and God's punishment for their sins.

Midas and Minerva considered other options beside wrapping and splinting Mercury's feet. They could send Mercury away to relatives in another community where Mercury's original family would not be revealed. But, what would being "an orphan" do to Mercury's emotional state? They knew already that they would be very lonesome without him.

Another option was to face up to their destiny and accept Mercury for what he is; but, they worried, would Mercury become maladjusted and ridiculed by the community in their disappointment?

What should be done?

Midas and Minerva made their decision, as true Mukies should. They were too large for worry, too noble for anger, too strong for fear, and too happy to permit the presence of trouble. They decided to accept and appreciate their "bud," Mercury, as he was. After all, Mercury was special and what may appear to be a handicap may actually be an "exceptional trait."

Midas and Minerva presented their Mercury to the community without apology or regret. Some members of the community did voice concern on how "unfortunate" Mercury was to be "handicapped," but most accepted Mercury's difference and his lot in life.

Mercury grew up "looking at the sunny side of everything and making his optimism come true by thinking only of the best, working only for the best, and expecting only the best." Oh sure, he tried to learn to walk and run like the other Mukies, but he was unsuccessful.

At first his peers laughed at the way Mercury walked and ran, but soon Mercury's ability to run fast overshadowed his difference in appearance. Mercury's so-called "handicap" became a big asset.

Because of his abnormally straight feet, Mercury became the fastest Mukie ever born. He won all contests and races and brought pride to his community. At a young age he became admired and respected throughout the Mukies' world.

Being different was better in other ways. Mercury was humble about his differences and was respected because he gave every living creature a smile and was so busy improving himself he had no time to criticize others.

The community's admiration of Mercury changed from his parent's physical attractiveness and heritage to respect for his service to others. In cases of community emergencies, Mercury was always the first to arrive. His handicap helped him rush to the aid of others, which he consistently did.

Would you prefer to be respected for your attractiveness, ancestors, or service to others?

"Mercury the handicapped" became "Mercury the great." This "cripple" became admired and respected for his unique talent and ability to excel, but most of all he was respected for his service and caring for others.

Which was Mercury's greatest gift? Why?

To Review:

1. Do you know anyone who is handicapped and has won fame and honor for his or her personal accomplishments?

2. Describe what Mercury's life may have been like had he been banished from the community. Describe the life his parents might have without him.

3. What options would Mercury's parents have regarding his physical handicap if this occurred in our present society?

4. Discuss how prestige is developed within a community and whether or not it is important.

5. How do you think his parents, grandparents, and neighbors treated Mercury? Are close family and friends important in how a person feels about himself?

6. Why do you think Mercury's optimistic attitude and caring were just as important as his ability to run fast?

Activities:

1. Think of some games in which Mercury could have excelled. In what games might he not been able to participate?

2. Role play a conversation within Mercury's home when it was first discovered that he had the talent to run faster than any other Mukie.

2. List ways of showing respect to others.

3. Give examples of respect and disrespect shown to the flag, the elderly, the police, the President, and others in public office.

4. Make a list of persons you respect and admire and give reasons why you do.

5. Make a list of ways classmates can show respect toward each other; toward their parents and teachers.

6. Explain what Mercury's parents did to help the community accept him. How can family members work together to take care of each other? Share answers with group.

7. With a partner, draw a picture of Mercury, with one person describing while the other draws.

8. Develop a list of famous athletes and state the importance of their having a postive, caring, and optimistic attitude.

Theme: The story "Guilt" provides the opportunity to discuss optimism and a positive outlook on life in contrast to pessimism and a negative viewpoint. It illustrates the reactions one has to another based on the mix of the parties' attitudes. It demonstrates the power of guilt and the saying: "It is better to be wronged than to wrong another."

This story introduces the concept of repentance and its influence upon those who suffer from guilt. It also gives insight into "punishment," its purpose, and degrees of severity.

Chapter 5

Guilt

Unfortunately, Mercer was born a true pessimist among a community of optimistic Mukies. As an infant he smiled very seldom and a frown was his most common expression. As a toddler, he envied others for their toys and apparent happiness. As he grew older, he wished that he had been born at a different time in a different place.

Mercer was critical of the success of others and had low self-esteem. Worst of all, he was unhappy and disliked people who appeared happy. Mercer was a very negative kid.

Do you know a pessimist? What do think can be done to change this attitude?

No one knew what made Mercer so negative. No one knew what to do to change him. The Mukies that knew him complimented him when he did something well and appeared enthusiastic about his success. They met him with a smile and did not criticize him. But still he was so unhappy and negative that everyone gave up on trying to change him. They took the attitude, "If it makes him happy to be unhappy, let him be unhappy, but not around me."

One day Mercer was playing a team sport called "OOPS" with a group of other Mukies. Maynard , Mercer's partner, was trying very hard to win; whereas, Mercer had given up because they were behind in the score. Maynard encouraged Mercer with positive comments on his playing but Mercer gave up, quit the game, and was walking away.

Maynard ran up to Mercer and said, "You can't quit. You're my partner and we can win." Mercer ignored Maynard and kept on walking.

Maynard lost his optimistic composure and gave Mercer a little shove. Mercer became overwhelmed with anger. This then turned to violence.

Mercer butted Maynard in the head and knocked him down. Mercer pounced on him and proceeded to keep hitting him. It was a painful sight. Others from the group had to pull Mercer off.

Some adult Mukies arrived on the scene after the attack had taken place. They only saw Maynard on the ground and Mercer being restrained by the other Mukies. They carried Maynard home and escorted Mercer to his home and told his parents that Mercer had beaten Maynard. They told Mercer's parents that Mercer's violence was unacceptable in the community. They were to bring Mercer in front of the elders of the community the next morning to receive his punishment sentence.

What do you think Mercer's punishment should be?

Maynard recovered from his injuries and was resting at home while Mercer was being sentenced by the elders. The elders said they would not tolerate unprovoked violence such as that was demonstrated by Mercer.

They asked Mercer to explain his side of the story. But from his pessimistic viewpoint, Mercer thought, "what good would it do?" and he remained silent. Mercer's silence angered the elders.

They pronounced that for three months Mercer should be confined to a room in his home without contact with any Mukie other than his father who would provide him with enough food to keep him alive. After this time Mercer would wear the letter "0" (which represents "offender") around his neck in public and no one would look at him, talk to him, or mention his name.

What do you think of this punishment?

When Maynard heard about the harsh punishment, he became very upset. He felt guilty because his shove of Mercer provoked Mercer's anger and attack. His guilt overwhelmed him. He had to do something to repent for what he had done even if it meant that he also would be punished.

There was an old Mukie saying, "It is better to be wronged than to wrong another."

What do you think this saying means?

The next day, Maynard went to the elders and confessed that he had provoked Mercer's anger and violence. The elders listened to Maynard's story and told him they would take the matter under advisement.

The elders were puzzled:

> Why didn't Mercer tell them that Maynard had provoked the incident by a physical push or shove?

> Why did Maynard shove Mercer in the first place?

Now the elders felt guilty because they acted in sentencing Mercer without having all the facts. They had to reconsider the degree of punishment in regard to its purpose and effect:

> Was the punishment to set an example to help prevent future violence in the community?

> Would the punishment rehabilitate Mercer's negative attitude?

> Should Maynard be punished for his part in the incident?

Now there were three parties involved and all were feeling guilty. Mercer perhaps felt guilty for the first time as he now realized that Maynard, Mercer's closest thing to a friend, cared enough about him to share the blame in an attempt to reduce Mercer's punishment. Maynard felt guilty because he had provoked the incident for which only Mercer was being punished. And the elders felt guilty for the severe punishment based on negative attitudes rather than the deed itself and deciding the punishment before gathering all the facts.

After much discussion, the elders came to the verdict. Mercer's punishment was reduced to one week isolation in his home and no wearing of the offender symbol. They sentenced Maynard to two days of isolation in the home. Both had to appear together before their peers and publicly apologize for their behavior.

Now, all parties involved had a means of repenting for their wrong doings.

To Review:

1. Discuss the role of "elders" and their importance in a family as well as in a community.

2. Discuss Mercer's negative attitude and possible reasons that it developed.

3. Discuss the importance of having an optimistic attitude.

4. Who influences the way a person's self-image is formed?

5. Discuss the saying, "Spend so much time improving yourself that you have no time to criticize others."

6. It takes courage to tell others that you were part of the wrong doing. Do you think Maynard would have been able to "live with himself" if he had not told the elders the part he played in the problem? Finish this scenario: Maynard did not tell the elders what he did. Everyday he walked past Mercer's house and knew that Mercer was being punished. The seat that Mercer sat in at school was empty. He didn't have anyone to walk with going home. What are other thoughts about how Maynard felt and what he did?

Activities:

1. Role-play other scenarios that may have developed if Maynard's behavior had been different.

2. How do you think Mercer should have handled his anger?

3. Some helpful ways of handling angry feelings might be to:
   a. Take a walk by yourself.
   b. Write down how you feel.
   c. Run, jog, swim, rollerblade, ride your bike, or do other forms of exercise.
   d. Play the piano or a musical instrument.
   e. Use art supplies, such as clay, and punch it or shape it, or paint or draw.
   f. Tell another uninvolved person how you feel.
   g. Have a good cry.

Complete the phrase, "When I get upset with the behavior of others I should..."

4. Relate a time and situation in which conflict arose because a person's behavior was not acceptable.

5. Debate the value of guilt in a society. One advocate that guilt is necessary in a caring society and the other advocate that guilt has little value and is detrimental to the emotional well-being.

6. Describe your interpretation of the following: "It is better to be wronged than to wrong another."

Theme: "The Mukies Change of Heart" introduces the concept of prejudices that can develop toward outsiders or foreigners by individuals in the community and the community as a whole. The outwardly display of distrust and anger impacts how the outsider feels. This creates long term effects and change is a time consuming and difficult process.

The story also examines the roles, moirés, and responsibilities of family members in the way they care for each other. It indicates how each member's self-esteem and attitude influence those around them. It demonstrates how only through example and open communication can a positive attitude and self-esteem be developed and maintained.

Chapter 6

The Mukies' Change of Heart

In the Mukie tradition, citizens married within their own villages. Mukies who were citizens of other villages were recognized as similar Mukies. But yet, these Mukies from other villages were viewed as being different and suspicious.

"Foreign" Mukies were welcomed to a village, but only as short-term guests and not as citizens with equal respect and trust. "Foreign" Mukies were thought to have beliefs and practices that over a period of time would corrupt or hurt the local community.

Who are "foreign" people in your life?

It was also a Mukie tradition that family responsibilities or duties were clear and respected. One such family custom was that the youngest son of the family had the duty to care for his aging parents. This meant that the youngest son lived with and supported his parents until they died.

This was the case with the youngest son, Merlin, of a family in the village of Myland. Merlin's older brothers and sisters had all married and left the home. The care of the elderly parents was left to him. At first he accepted these responsibilities, but after a while he became restless and tired of his duties.

Merlin wanted to experience life outside his home and even his village of Myland. One day he decided to leave his home and village. He traveled to a far off village of Bosue where jobs were promising and he was independent. Here he found a job and sought a different life without the responsibility to his parents.

Was this okay?

At work Merlin met a woman Mukie named Bodo. They became friends and fell in love. Although he was not fully accepted, Merlin was content in Bosue, but the guilt created by neglecting his duty for his parents grew.

What makes one feel guilty?

Merlin realized that as the youngest male of the family he had the responsibility for the care of his elderly parents, and that he needed to return to his own village of Myland. However, he feared that the one he loved and his wife-to-be, Bodo, would have difficulty being accepted by his family and the citizens of Myland. She loved Merlin, but there were many obstacles or problems to overcome before she would give up her family and the safety of her home community.

Bodo was shy and cautious and she lacked confidence in her ability to adapt to his community. She was afraid they would not accept her. Bodo was a pessimist who thought the worst things would happen. But, their mutual love for each other became stronger. They decided to make the life-long vows of marriage to each other.

Merlin and Bodo were married according to the customs of her community of Bosue. The ceremony and vows were different from Merlin's community but the married couple's love made them too large for worry, too noble for anger, too strong for fear, and too happy to permit the presence of trouble.

Soon after they were married, Merlin decided that they should return to his village of Myland. When they returned to Myland the couple received a cool reception. Merlin's family was angry that he left his duties and that he married a foreigner.

Should the relatives be angry?

His relatives' anger with him for neglecting their parents soon turned to his foreign wife, Bodo. In their minds, she became the one who prevented Merlin from fulfilling his duties to his parents and to them.

Have you ever blamed someone for what the one you love did?

Soon Bodo thought that not only the entire village viewed her as an "outsider" but that they suspected her of different and secret activities and influences on their lives. Later, even the deaths of his parents, although completely unfounded, were associated with Bodo's mere presence. The relatives blamed her for all the family misfortune. Rumors of her mistakes of the past were created, exaggerated, and related to things that happened now in Myland.

Bodo felt accused, misunderstood and condemned. Attitudes or feelings of Merlin's relatives as well as the coolness of other citizens of the community caused her to stay at home by herself.

When you think people dislike you what do you do?

Bodo viewed herself as a community outcast and felt that only Merlin had any interest or concern for her. She became more pessimistic, gloomy, and negative. These attitudes caused her to feel dirty and sinful. She was critical of herself and developed severe guilt.

Even the birth of their son, Myrong, did not help in Bodo's social acceptance and self-concept. It only provided further opportunity for her isolation, self-blame, and feeling of self-pity.

Bobo was living a gloomy life that made her pessimism come true. She lived preparing for criticism or neglect rather than thinking for the best, working for the best, and expecting the best.

The success of others was humbling or belittling to Bobo. It made her feel inferior. Not being social and involved in the community prevented her from excelling at or doing anything. But her isolation lessened her fear of failure and criticism.

How do you feel when your friends do well?

Merlin found relief from pessimism and gloom in his job. He worked from sun up to sun down. He knew little about his son because of his dedication to his work.

Was this what Merlin should do?

Myrong grew up in the shadow of pessimism created by his mother. However, as he matured the idea of being inferior, guilty, dirty, and rejected became less. Myrong was not the brightest or most talented Mukie in the community, but he tried hard and he succeeded. Even though he had to work harder and longer to accomplish tasks, he developed an optimistic attitude.

The successes of Myrong turned his Mother's pessimism into his own optimism. He forgot the mistakes of the past and sought achievements and accomplishments in the future. He was so busy improving himself, he had no time to neither be critical of others nor fear the criticism of others. In fact, he became enthusiastic about the success of others, which in turn increased the number of friends he had and people who cared.

Always looking for the sunny side of everything made Myrong's optimism come true! He listened more than he spoke and let nothing disturb his positive outlook on life.

Are these things difficult to accomplish?

This optimistic outlook spread not only to Myrong's friends but also most importantly to his parents, especially his mother. The years of Bodo's isolation and pessimism were past but the toll they took on her and those around her remained. It was difficult to forget the mistakes of the past and press on the achievements of the present and future.

Bobo took pride in their son's accomplishments but still feared criticism and lacked self-confidence. However, she learned to make the best of what she had and worked to over-come her insecurity. With the model of their son, she and Merlin found a new life and respect of the community.

Those in the community slowly learned that you cannot judge a person by how they look or from where they come. They also learned there are many factors that determine why persons act the way they do. These often remain unseen.

Have you ever had difficulty forgetting and forgiving your own or the mistakes of others in the past?

To Review:

1. What are some characteristics of others that could make them "different" and therefore could be subject to prejudice by some people?

2. Discuss the characteristics of a foreigner and the anxiety they sometimes create in a community.

3. Do you think Bodo should have gone back to her own community? Why or why not?

4. Discuss how Bodo's self-imposed isolation enhanced the community's negative attitude toward her.

5. Discuss how Bodo's self-concept deteriorated because she had no one to listen to her.

6. One of the Mukies' custom was that the youngest son of the family cared for his aging parents. Can you think of other customs that may be common in families? Do some children attend the same university or college as their parents? Are some children expected to go into the same type of business as their parents? Do some families celebrate certain holidays a particular way?

7. How would you feel if Merlin had not come back to his own community to care for his parents? How do you think Merlin would have felt?

8. Do you think that pessimism and optimism are inherited characteristics or are they a learned or acquired trait?

Activities:

1. Find out whether there is a new student in your school or neighborhood. Try to find out what this student's greatest fear was upon entering a new school or neighborhood?

2. Role play a situation in which the topic is the acceptance of a "foreigner" into a group.

3. Develop a list of other's behaviors that caused Bodo to develop a low self-concept and guilt.

4. Role play Bodo and a listener as she talks about her concerns, observations, and worries.

5. Although Merlin was busy from sun up to sun down, give suggestions on how he could help his wife and son feel they were loved, important, and not neglected.

Theme: "A Mukie of a Different Color" examines a situation of racial minority and the attitudes that develop in the minds of both parties involved. It shows how biases can inhibit impartial judgments. Biases create prejudices or preconceived and unreasonable attitudes. Prejudices may be found in a wide variety of circumstances such as age, religion, gender, nationalities, occupations, and race.

This story examines racial bias before it becomes a prejudice in a very basic and specific situation—a single young purple Mukie among a large peer group of brown Mukies. The purple colored Mukie's identity was first one of curiosity, then distrust, and finally indifference.

Ignoring someone and demonstrating a non-caring attitude is more painful than verbal abuse or name-calling. In the minds of the discriminated ones, self-esteem diminishes and the awareness that one has little or no influence upon others or the situation becomes an obsession.

This story points out the importance of caring associations — friends. In this story, a single event changes the mental perspectives of those involved. However, there are "fences to be mended" before mutual acceptance, respect, and friendships can develop.

Chapter 7

A Mukie of a Different Color

Manchester was born with purple hair body covering. As you know, Mukies are "naturally" brown with black tipped hair covering and dark brown eyes. But Manchester Mukie had purple body hair and pink eyes like his father's hair and eyes. Manchester's mother was a "natural" Mukie color. Manchester and his father were the only purple Mukies in the community. Manchester's facial features and stature were much the same as the other Mukies, and his mind was as keen and his heart as caring as other Mukies.

Do you know someone with skin a different color from yours?

Early in life Manchester realized that he looked different from the other Mukies of the community, but he was satisfied that he looked like his father. He would say to himself, "Sure I am different, but it's ok." He never asked, "Why me?" but instead said "Why not me? I can handle it." After all, Manchester was an optimistic Mukie: too large for worry, too noble for anger, too strong for fear, and too happy to permit the presence of trouble.

However, as Manchester grew older, socialization with the other Mukies and their friendship became essential to him. The views of others his age became very, very important. His contentment with only looking like his father grew less. He became unhappy and disappointed with his lot in life.

How important are friends in your life?

At first Manchester noticed the other Mukies looked at him curiously. Then he thought their looks indicated their distrust of him. Later, he detected the look of fear when they looked at him. And finally he saw the look of indifference or a non-caring attitude on the part of the other Mukies. They ignored him. They moved away when he came near. Sometimes they would even avoid looking at him or speaking to him.

Have you ever had the feeling that someone didn't care anything about you? How did you feel?

Manchester felt isolated and alone without anyone but his parents to care for him. He became an unhappy pessimist. His cheerful countenance and peace of mind turned into frowns of despair, anxiety, and frustration. How much of the other Mukies' non-caring attitudes were created in Manchester's mind and how much were real, we do not know. But Manchester would isolate himself and watch the other Mukies play from a distance, hoping perhaps someone would ask him to join them.

Do you know anyone who acts like Manchester? Do you know anyone who acts like the other Mukies?

Now the Mukies had only one natural predator or enemy; that was the yellow-bellied, two-headed boa constrictor snake. It was a huge, long creature, yellow-red in color, and could devour two entire Mukies at a time. Although the Mukies were usually too strong for fear and too happy to permit the presence of trouble, these creatures terrified them. Even hearing about them made their legs shake and their ears ring. Who knows what would happen if they ever saw one!

Do you fear any creatures?

One day Manchester was walking by an area where a large group of other Mukies his own age was playing a game. Manchester was standing at a distance watching the Mukies and probably wishing they would invite him to play. As he stood there he heard a rustling in the grass some distance away. He looked up and saw the two heads of a boa constrictor slithering through the grass toward the Mukies who were playing.

What do you think he should do?

Manchester ran toward the group as fast as his short stocky legs would carry him. In this time of trouble, he forgot the hurt caused by the indifference of others.

He yelled as loud as he could, "Run for your lives!"

Recall that the group usually ignored Manchester. This time, too, the group continued to play, until they saw the two heads sticking above the grass coming their way.

There was yelling, panic, and chaos among the group as they scattered and ran in all directions. As the others ran, Manchester stood in the path of the oncoming snake.

When the snake saw Manchester, it stopped, turned, and retreated.

What neither Manchester nor the other Mukies knew was that the snake feared the color purple. You see, the snake's worst enemy and predator was the purple hawk. It feared any creature that resembled the dreaded purple hawk. And to the snake, Manchester's purple coloring was like that of its own worst enemy.

Manchester became an immediate hero in the community. He had saved the children from a terrible fate.

To Review:

1. Discuss Manchester's change in attitude and behavior as he grew older and the need for friends to listen to him became more important.

2. What are some of the problems of judging other people by the color of their skin?

3. What are common prejudices and how are they developed?

4. What is meant by "indifference?" Give an example.

5. Discuss how being negative toward someone or toward what he/she does is sometimes better than being indifferent or not caring.

6. Discuss cliques and the intentional exclusion of others in a group.

7. What do you think Manchester's parents told him about the color of his skin when he was a little child and questioning them about it?

8. Discuss what Manchester and the group of Mukies must have thought and said when the snake turned and retreated.

9. Do you think Manchester will now be included in other children's games? Why or why not?

Activities:

1. Role play a conversation between Manchester and his parents when they talked about rejection from the other Mukies.

2. Role play a situation in which one or two of the group thanked Manchester for his brave behavior.

3. Find quotes about friendships. Share with others.

4. Being a good friend means being a good listener. List 5 good listening suggestions.

5. Role play Manchester and a friend who listens effectively to Manchester's expressed concerns about his acceptance.

6. Instead of anger, hatred, and violence, which sometime accompany prejudices, how would you like to see differences handled in the real world? Share with the group.

7. Each add a conclusion to how you think Manchester will now be treated.

Theme: "The Honey Tree" is an example of how violence and war-like actions can erupt even in a society of happy, loving, and caring individuals such as the Mukies. It points out the importance of mutual trust and open discussion in which people really listen to each side of the story. When distrust escalates and misunderstanding becomes group protest, conflicts become harder to resolve. And rumors can magnify and add to the problems.

This story shows how one person can make a difference. This person believed that individual actions and behavior were more important than violence. Where once there was hatred, chaos, and discord, he felt love and peace can abide. The story also provides an opportunity for the reader and listener to help solve the problem inherent in the story.

Chapter 8

The Honey Tree

As we know, the Mukies by nature were optimistic and happy creatures. But, sometimes circumstances created within them less than optimistic attitudes. In other words, some Mukies and even entire communities of Mukies became disheartened and upset with others and even with themselves. They lost faith, respect, and trust. When this occurred, the end results were war-like feelings and actions.

Have you ever lost respect for and trust of a person?

The communities of Mukieville and Mukiedale were located in the same geographical region and bordered each other. They had a long history of living together in peace. The border was not clearly marked and that really didn't matter until the tree indicating the boundary became valuable. A large swarm of honeybees chose this particular tree for their hives. It was then that the tree and the border created a dispute between the two communities. You see, next to melilot, honey was their favorite food.

Why would these circumstances create a dispute?

The leaders, the elders of the communities, argued about the rights of each other's community to the honey. Each accused the other's citizens of sneaking and stealing the honey that rightfully belonged to their community. The two communities' leaders became so angry at each other that hatred developed and threats of violence occurred.

Unfortunately, hatred and distrust developed within each community as well as against the other community. The citizens of both communities became insecure, anxious, and suspicious of others. Families became self-centered and isolated themselves even from their neighbors.

One warm summer evening four Mukieville citizens decided to raid the honey for their own private benefit. After all, they reasoned, the main entrance to the hive was on the Mukieville side of the tree. They figured they had as much right to the honey as any citizen from Mukiedale.

The raiders got caught in the act by several citizens of Mukiedale. They were captured, taken prisoners, and brought to a makeshift cage used as a jail.

The message that four citizens of Mukieville were being held captive spread rapidly throughout their community. False rumors were spread about their capture and the way they were being treated.

Have you ever been aware of or were influenced by rumors?

The rumors, although unfounded, stirred the hearts and minds of the once happy and carefree Mukieville citizens to anger and hatred. They became divided in their public protesting. One group wanted immediate retaliation for the capture of their citizens by declaring war against their neighbor. Another group thought there should be some official, but non-violent, action taken against the Mukiedales for their role in the affair.

Have you ever let anger become violent behavior?

The Mukiedale citizens, too, were publicly protesting, but they were angered by the apparent invasion of what they considered their property — namely, the honey tree. Violence erupted among the public protestors in both communities. Unfortunately, the louder, noisier groups who wanted to wage war influenced their leaders to take action. Each began to prepare for war.

The young men in both communities were called upon to train for battle. They used clubs as weapons and helmets for "head butting." The Mukies had never heard of guns or bombs, or even bows and arrows. Even if the bow and arrow had been invented, they couldn't have used them because of their short chunky arms and less than mobile hands and fingers. They didn't even know how or why to swing a club at a fellow Mukie. It was not in their nature to harm another living being. Remember, the Mukies did not even eat the flesh of other creatures. They were a peace-loving society.

It took time to prepare for combat since this was a new concept for the Mukies – they had never before gone to war. While the armies were being formed and the protestors continued to protest, the leaders stalled for time. They were indifferent as to why the conflict occurred in the first place.

There was a young man in Mukiedale, Francis was his name, who did not believe in public protest nor in violence, combat, or war. He firmly believed that the individual was too noble for anger, too strong for fear, and too happy to permit trouble to develop. He strove to be so strong that nothing could disturb the peace he felt in his heart and mind. He did not criticize others, but only concentrated on improving himself. For this attitude, Francis was highly respected in his community. Nevertheless, he was called to train to fight for the honor of his community that had been invaded.

Do you think that one individual can make a difference and influence a community?

Francis loved his community and was loyal to its causes, but he didn't think he knew all the facts about the invasion. He was opposed to violence and he believed that each individual citizen could influence a community more by his/her own actions and behavior than by group protest or violence. Francis asked and received permission to visit with the elders of his Mukiedale community.

At the meeting, Francis did not judge his elders nor did he criticize their decision to prepare for war. He merely said:

My wish is that peace may begin with me.
Where there is hatred, may I create love.
Where there is discord, may I create unity.
Where there is doubt, may I have faith.
Where there is falsehood, may I find truth.
Where there ignorance, may I find learning.
Where there is despair, may I create hope.
Where there is sadness, may I bring joy.
May I realize that it is not as important to be understood,
*   as it is to understand, and to be loved, as it is to love.*
May I realize that it is in giving that I receive, and in pardoning
*   that I am pardoned.*

Adapted from the Prayer of St. Francis of Assisi

The Mukiedale elders listened in silence and awe. They were so impressed by Francis' sincerity and optimism that they adopted his wish as their own.

Do you think that you could live by that creed?

They discussed Francis' wish with the elders from the opposing community. They, too, chose to adopt his wish as the rules of their community. Peace, love, unity, faith, truth, learning, hope, and joy were to abound.

In regard to their mutual problem of the honey raid, the elders all agreed. They decided to judge and sentence the four prisoners for their individual selfish motives rather than as representatives of any community.

Do you think this was a wise decision? Why or why not?

No, the ownership of the honey tree problem was not immediately resolved. But this, too, the elders decreed to settle by negotiation rather than by violent action. Just as Francis did, they came to believe that the individual was too noble for anger, too strong for fear, and too happy to permit trouble to develop.

How would you settle the honey ownership problem?

To Review:

1. What created the boundary line between the two communities?

2. How can distrust lead to conflict?

3. Discuss the rights and responsibilities of an individual in a community's aggressive action, such as war.

4. What is meant by "negotiation?"

5. How can rumors create conflict?

6. What are alternatives to violence and war?

7. What do you suggest the Mukies could have done that would have helped ease or lessen the problem before it escalated into group protest?

8. Discuss the ways an individual may express his /her opinions or attitudes in regard to a community's policy or action.

9. Why do you think the Mukies were able to live without conflicts for long periods of time?

Activities:

1. Point out selfish motives on the part of each community.

2. Role play the leaders of the two communities negotiating the rights for the honey tree.

3. Role play a conversation among the four Mukies who conspired and enacted the theft of the honey.

4. Give an example of situations throughout history where one person's decision made a difference in the lives of others.

5. Write a summary of how you think the problem of the honey tree should be handled.

6. With a partner, draw a picture of the honey tree as one describes the tree while the other draws. Then take turns.

7. Re-read the saying of St. Francis and discuss how one might enact the wishes in a family, community, and/or nation.

8. Write your poem or story entitled: "I Can Make a Difference."

About the Author

Robert Bohlken, Ph.D., Professor Emeritus of Communication , retired after 42 years of teaching at both the secondary and university levels and is currently a communication consultant and author. His professional areas of expertise and research are in listening, semantics, and interpersonal trust/relationship. He has published more than twenty academic journal articles, presented papers at more than forty academic conferences, made more than sixty service and social club presentations, and authored three booklets: *Grandpa Listens as Bobby Grows Up*, *How the Rabbit Became the Easter Bunny*, and *How to Talk Rural Northwest Missouri Talk*.

Dr. Bohlken is a member of the International Listening Association, International Society of General Semantics, National Communication Association, and a life member of the Optimist International Service Club. He is a Korean War veteran and has been a long-time member of the American Legion.

Degrees held by Dr. Bohlken include a B.S. in Language Arts Education with Distinction, Nebraska State College, Peru; Master of Arts Degree in Communication/Theatre Arts, University of Nebraska; and Doctorate of Philosophy in Communication, University of Kansas, Lawrence.